silly Millies

What Do You Do at the

ZOO?

Susan E. Goodman

Illustrated by Steve Pica

The Millbrook Press
Brookfield, Connecticut

To my book group—here's one we can all finish.

Copyright © 2002 by Susan E. Goodman
Illustrations copyright © 2002 by Steve Pica

Reading Consultant: Lea M. McGee

Silly Millies and the Silly Millies logo are trademarks of
The Millbrook Press, Inc.

Library of Congress Cataloging-in-Publication Data
Goodman, Susan E.
What do you do— at the zoo? / Susan E. Goodman ; illustrated by Steve Pica.
p. cm. — (Silly Millies)
Summary: Having been asked by the zookeeper to help feed and care
for various zoo animals, a boy discovers a variety of facts about their diet
and behavior as he helps each one.
ISBN 0-7613-2755-X (lib. binding) ISBN 0-7613-1787-2 (pbk.)
[1. Zoo animals—Fiction.] I. Title: What do you do at the zoo?.
II. Pica, Steve, ill. III. Title. IV. Series.
PZ7.G61444 Wf 2002   [E]—dc21   2001006481

Published by The Millbrook Press, Inc.
2 Old New Milford Road
Brookfield, Connecticut 06804
www.millbrookpress.com

The zookeeper needs help.

"Please feed the lion," she says.

What do you do?

You huff and puff.
The lion eats a lot of meat.
It could eat 70 pounds of meat
for lunch.

You want to feed the baby camel.
But here comes its mother.
What do you do?

Back off!

Mothers want to keep their
babies safe.

Mother camels kick hard.

The giraffes do not have
much water.

What do you do?

Nothing.

Giraffes do not drink much water.

They get it in their food.

15

The elephants drink a lot of water.

What do you do?

Grab the hose.

And put on a raincoat.

Elephants might spray you—

just for fun.

19

The monkeys need some fun, too.
What do you do?

You hide their food.
Monkeys love to play hide-
and-seek.

Oh no! The hippo is in the pool.
It has not come up for air.
What do you do?

Wait.

Hippos can stay under water for five minutes.

The day is over.

The zookeeper is happy.

"Thank you!" she says.

What do you do?

30

Say "You're welcome," of course!

Dear Parents:

Congratulations! By sharing this book with your child, you are taking an important step in helping him or her become a good reader. *What Do You Do at the Zoo?* is perfect for the child who can read with help. Below are some ideas for making sure your child's reading experience is a positive one.

TIPS FOR READING

- If your child knows most of the alphabet, begin by reading the book aloud, pausing every page or so to talk about the pictures. Point to the words as you read. When your child is familiar with the book, pause before the end of a sentence to see if your child will supply the word. Play word and letter games. For example, have your child point to words that begin with the same letter of the alphabet. Or write a word from the book on a card and see if your child can find it in the book.
- If your child knows how to read some words and knows the "sounds" of some letters, invite your child to read aloud to you. If your child does not know a word or reads it incorrectly, help by asking "What word do you think it will be?" or "Does that word make sense?" Encourage your child to look to the pictures for word clues. Or point to the first letter (or first two letters) of the word. If your child is stumped, pronounce the word slowly, running your finger underneath the letters.
- Encourage your child to reread the book. This builds confidence and gradually your child will be able to read without your help. Remember to provide lots of praise for the hard work of your early reader.

TIPS FOR DISCUSSION

- Talk about your last visit to the zoo. What did your child learn about the zoo during that visit? What did your child learn by reading? Talk about different ways to learn about animals.
- Can your child name more animals that might live in a zoo? How is a zoo animal's life different from life in it's natural environment? What are the good and bad things about living in a zoo?

Lea M. McGee, Ed.D.
Professor, Literacy Education
University of Alabama